For Cooper, Emily and Emily, who love Christmas more than any family I know. – B.T.

To my amazing Mum and Dad x – S.R.

Farshore

First published in Great Britain 2021 by Farshore

An imprint of HarperCollins*Publishers*
1 London Bridge Street, London SE1 9GF
www.farshorebooks.com

HarperCollins*Publishers*
1st Floor, Watermarque Building, Ringsend Road
Dublin 4, Ireland

Text copyright © Barry Timms 2021
Illustrations copyright © Siân Roberts 2021
Barry Timms and Sian Roberts have asserted their moral rights.

ISBN 978 0 00 849899 3
Printed in the UK by Pureprint a CarbonNeutral® company
1

A CIP catalogue record for this title is available from the British Library.

MIX
Paper from
responsible sources
FSC
www.fsc.org
FSC™ C007454

This book is produced from independently certified FSC™ paper to ensure responsible forest management.

For more information visit: www.harpercollins.co.uk/green

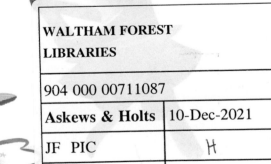

This book was printed in the UK by a CarbonNeutral® company, using vegetable-based inks.

The TWELVE GREEN DAYS of CHRISTMAS

Barry Timms · Siân Roberts

Farshore

On the first day of Christmas,
what did Santa see?

A star that had broken in three.

On the second day of
Christmas, what did
Santa see?

Two tattered gloves

and a star that had
broken in three.

On the third day of Christmas,
what did Santa see?

Three crushed cups,
two tattered gloves
and a star that had broken in three.

On the fourth day of Christmas –
now what could it be?

Four party hats,

three crushed cups,
two tattered gloves
and a star that had
broken in three.

On the fifth day of Christmas,

goodness gracious me . . .

. . . FIVE
worn-out wings!

Four party hats,
three crushed cups,
two tattered gloves
and a star that had
broken in three.

On the sixth day of Christmas,
Santa cried,

"ENOUGH!

It's time we recycled this stuff."

Dear forest friends,

Let's tidy up
and make this
the GREENEST
Christmas ever!

Love, Santa

On the seventh day of Christmas –
one **almighty storm!**

Poor Santa just
couldn't keep warm.

Atchoo!

forest friends,

t's tidy up
ake this
ENEST
s ever!

Santa

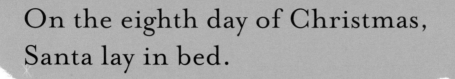

On the eighth day of Christmas,
Santa lay in bed.

And outside the rubbish just spread.

On the ninth day of Christmas –
what a dreadful dream!

Would Christmas EVER be green?

And the tenth day?
A junk pile!
Stretching to the sky . . .

But look what came
fluttering by!

On the eleventh day
of Christmas, a special
card arrived . . .

It made Santa tingle inside.

Dear Santa,

Get well soon!

We have a surprise for you when you're better.

Love,
Your forest friends

On the twelfth day of Christmas, what did Santa see . . . ?

Twelve crows collecting,

eleven squirrels sorting,
ten rabbits rinsing,

nine foxes fixing,
eight rats reusing,

seven hedgehogs heaving,
six beavers building . . .

BRAND NEW BINS!

Four clever birds,

three brave friends,

two
little
shoves ...

. . . and a star at
the top of the tree!